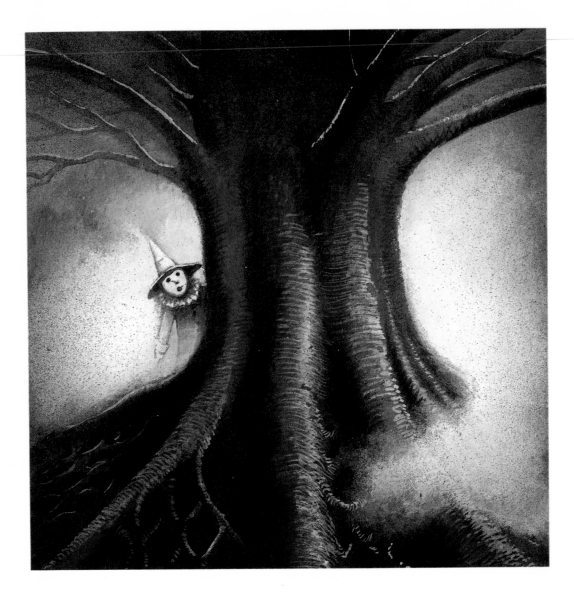

IT HARDLY SEEMS
LIKE HALLOWEEN

David S. Rose

Lothrop, Lee & Shepard Books • New York

Library of Congress Cataloging in Publication Data. Rose,
David S., (date) It hardly seems like Halloween. Summary:
Oblivious to the strange creatures gathering behind him,
a little boy complains that this Halloween is very dull.
[1. Halloween—Fiction] I. Title.
PZ7.R7148It 1983 [E] 83-750
ISBN 0-688-02092-5 ISBN 0-688-02093-3 (lib. bdg.)

To my daughters
Amanda
and
Alexis

Tonight is Halloween,

but it's not at all
what I expected.

There's not an owl
or black cat to be seen.

I had visions of scarecrows

wearing pumpkins,

and dwarfs

parading with munchkins.

Where are all the wizards

and terrible lizards

prowling

the dark with wicked witches?

I'd hoped there'd be ghosts

and beasts

and lots of scary things

that go screech in the night.

But there's not an eerie creature

to be seen.

It hardly seems like Halloween!